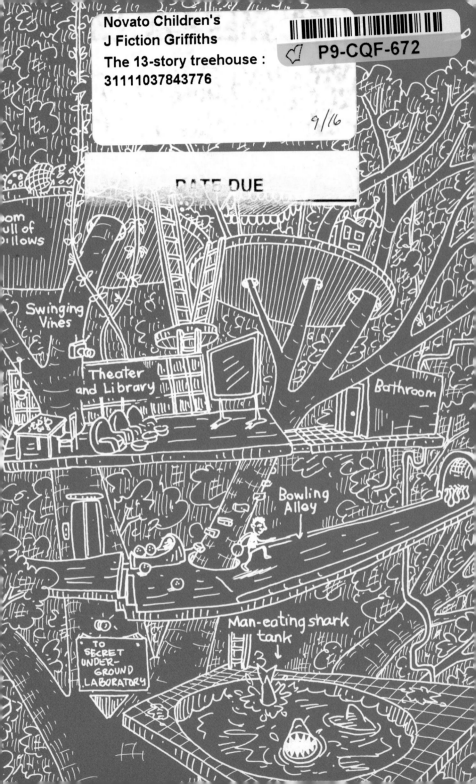

THE 13-STORY TREEHOUSE

ANDY GRIFFITHS

illustrated by Terry Denton

Feiwel and Friends • New York

A FEIWEL AND FRIENDS BOOK
An Imprint of Macmillan

Feiwel and Friends books may be purchased for business or promotional use.
For information on bulk purchases, please contact the Macmillan Corporate
and Premium Sales Department at (800) 221-7945 x5442 or by e-mail at
specialmarkets@macmillan.com.

Library of Congress Cataloging-in-Publication Data Available
ISBN: 978-1-250-02690-3 (hardcover)/978-1-250-04239-2 (ebook)

Book design by Katie Cline

Feiwel and Friends logo designed by Filomena Tuosto

Originally published as The 13-Storey Treehouse
in Australia by Pan Macmillan Australia Pty Ltd

First published in the United States by Feiwel and Friends,
an imprint of Macmillan

First U.S. Edition: 2013

20 19 18 17 16 15 14

mackids.com

CONTENTS

CHAPTER 1

THE 13-STORY TREEHOUSE

Hi, my name is Andy.

This is my friend Terry.

We live in a tree.

Well, when I say "tree," I mean treehouse. And when I say "treehouse," I don't mean any old treehouse— I mean a *13-story* treehouse!

So what are you waiting for?
Come on up!

It's got a bowling alley,

a see-through swimming pool,

a tank full of man-eating sharks,

vines you can swing on,

a games room,

a secret underground laboratory,

a lemonade fountain,

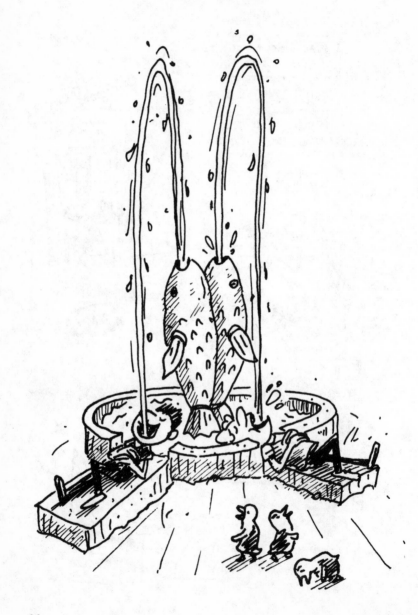

a vegetable vaporizer,

and a marshmallow machine that follows you around and automatically shoots marshmallows into your mouth whenever you're hungry.

As well as being our home, the treehouse is also where we make books together. I write the words and Terry draws the pictures.

As you can see, we've been
doing this for quite a while now.

CHAPTER 2

THE FLYING CAT

If you're like most of our readers, you're probably wondering where we get all the ideas for our books from. Well, sometimes we think them up. Other times they are based on stuff that actually happened. Like *this* book, for instance.

It all started one morning when I got up and went down to get some breakfast.

Terry was already in the kitchen. He was painting a cat. And when I say "painting a cat," I don't mean he was painting a *picture* of a cat. He was painting an *actual* cat! Bright yellow!

"This might be a stupid question, Terry," I said, "but why are you painting that cat bright yellow?"

"Because I'm turning it into a canary," he answered.

I started to explain to Terry that you can't turn a cat into a canary just by painting it yellow but he said, "Yes, you can—watch this!" and carried the dripping cat to the edge of the deck.

"No!" I yelled, as Terry held the cat out in mid-air . . . and let it go.

But I needn't have worried. The cat didn't fall.
Two little wings popped out of its back, and then
it tweeted and flew away.

"See?" said Terry, turning to me in triumph.
"I told you so!"

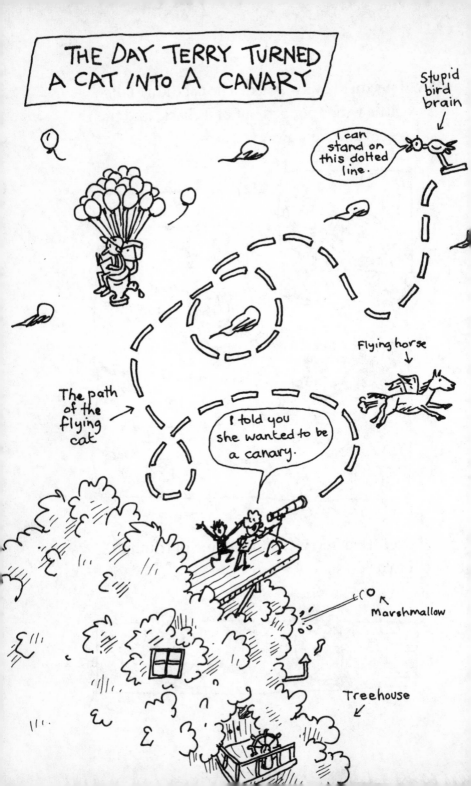

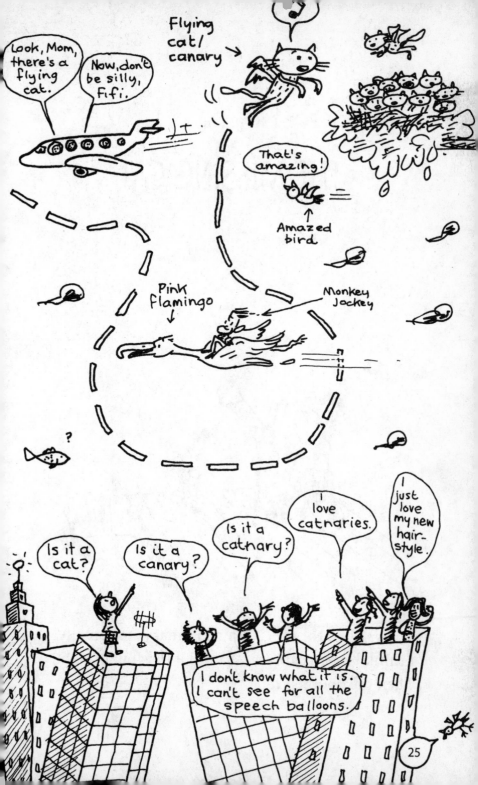

CHAPTER 3

THE MISSING CAT

We watched the cat . . . I mean canary . . . actually, I think I mean *catnary* . . . until it flew out of sight. Then the doorbell rang.

It was Jill, our neighbor. She lives on the other side of the forest in a house full of animals. She's got two dogs, a goat, three horses, four goldfish, one cow, six rabbits, two guinea pigs, one camel, one donkey, and one cat.

"Uh-oh," said Terry. "She's probably looking for her cat!"

"Don't tell me that was *Silky* you just turned into a canary!" I said.

"Okay, I won't," said Terry. "But it was."

This was bad. Jill loved that cat. She loved all her animals, but she especially loved Silky.

"Oh no!" I said. "She is going to be really mad when she finds out what you've done!"

"Maybe we shouldn't tell her."

"Good idea!" I said. "Let's pretend we're not home."

We did our best to lay low,
but it's pretty hard to hide
in a treehouse.

"It's no use hiding,"
called Jill. "I can hear you.
And I can *see* you.
Silky's gone missing
and I was wondering
if you'd seen her."

"No," I said quickly, "she's not here."

Now, before you start thinking I'm the kind of person who would tell a lie, I'd just like to point out that although the first part of my sentence ("No") was *technically* a lie, the second part ("she's not here") was *definitely* the truth, which—I'm sure you will agree—cancels out the lie.

"Oh," said Jill sadly. "Well, anyway, I've made up a missing-cat poster. Can I put one on your tree?"

"Sure," I said. "It's the least we can do." (Which was also definitely 100 percent true.)

MISSING CAT!
SILKY

she looks like this →

cute little ears ←

beautiful green eyes →

← darling whiskers

very soft white fur →

Likes: cat food. cuddles cats on TV

Dislikes: dogs, water, fleas, locked cat flaps.

BIG REWARD!! call JILL

As soon as Jill left I turned to Terry. "We've *got* to find that cat!" I said.

"You mean *canary*," said Terry.

"Whatever!" I said. "We've got to find her."

But before we could even begin looking for her the video-phone rang. (Yes, we've got one of those as well—and it's 3D!)

"Maybe that's Silky now," said Terry.

"Don't be stupid," I said. "Cats can't use phones."

"Maybe they can," said Terry. "You said they couldn't turn into canaries and you were wrong about that!"

CHAPTER 4

THE BIG RED NOSE

We raced back upstairs. A big red nose filled the video-phone screen. Uh-oh. It was Mr. Big Nose, our publisher. And he was angry. I could tell this because his nose was even bigger—and redder—than usual.

"WHERE'S MY BOOK?" he yelled.

"What book?" said Terry.

"The one you chuckle-heads promised me a year ago would be on my desk last Friday!"

"Oh," said Terry. "Is it last Friday already?"

"It's PAST last Friday already!" shouted Mr. Big Nose. "WAY past, and your book is STILL not on my desk."

The truth was we'd kind of forgotten about the book. We were a little behind schedule. Well, when I say "a little behind schedule," I mean a *lot* behind schedule. And when I say "a *lot* behind schedule," I mean a *LOT LOT LOT* behind schedule.

Not that I was about to let Mr. Big Nose know that. He was already pretty angry and the angrier he gets, the bigger his nose gets. And if his nose got any bigger I was worried that it might explode. And that was not something I wanted to see— especially not in 3D.

ABOVE: *An artist's impression of what it would look like if Mr. Big Nose's nose exploded.*

"No problem, Mr. Big Nose," I lied. "It's under control. We'll get it to you as soon as we can."

"Well, *as soon as you can* had better be by five o'clock tomorrow afternoon, or else!"

"Don't worry, Mr. Big Nose," I said. "It will be there, all right. You can count on us!"

"But—" said Terry.

I quickly ended the call before Terry could say anything that would make Mr. Big Nose any angrier than he already was.

"You shouldn't have told him that," said Terry. "I'm way too busy to get it done by tomorrow. Look at my 'To Do' list. I'm full up!"

"And don't even get me started on my 'To Don't' list."

"Your 'To Dos' and 'To Don'ts' will just have to wait," I said. "If we don't get this book finished it will be back to the monkey house for us."

"The monkey house?" said Terry, looking terrified. "Not the monkey house! *Anything* but the monkey house!"

For those of you who don't know, the monkey house is where Terry and I used to work. It was the worst job ever.

Cleaning the monkey house was bad enough . . .

grooming the monkeys was even worse . . .

but the worst job of all was having to fill in for the monkeys while they were on a break.

"I'm *not* going back to the monkey house," said Terry, "and that's final!"

"And you won't have to," I said, "not if we get our book finished. Come on, let's get started. We've only got until tomorrow!"

CHAPTER 5

THE DRAWING COMPETITION

We went to the kitchen table. It's where we do most of our work. Or, rather, in the case of the past year it's where we *didn't* do most of our work.

But that could soon be fixed. I figured Terry would have a few funny sketches in his drawing folder to get us started. It would simply be a matter of grabbing the best ones, adding a few words and, hey presto, we'd have our new book. No sweat, no worry. We are professional book-writers after all. I mean, you saw our pile of books on page 18.

JUST IN CASE YOU SKIPPED PG. 18
THIS IS WHAT IT LOOKED LIKE.

"Okay," I said, "let's see what you've got!"

Terry opened his drawing folder and laid it flat on the table. "You're going to love this," he said.

In front of me was a picture of a finger.

"This is just a picture of a finger," I said.

"Yes," said Terry proudly. "But not just *any* finger . . . it's *my* finger."

"Uh-huh," I said. "What else have you got?"

"I've got a *close-up* picture of my finger," said Terry. "And it's labeled."

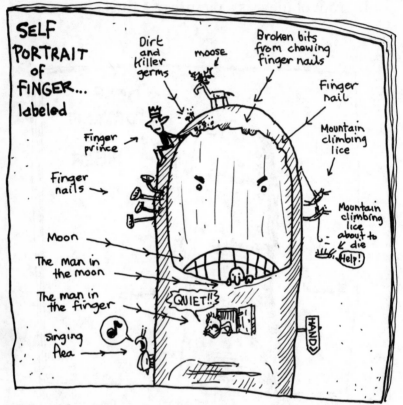

I stared at it.

"Well?" said Terry, a big grin on his face. "What do you think? *Lice* picks, get it? Not *ice* picks . . . *lice* picks!"

"Yeah, I get it," I said. I turned the pages, looking for more pictures, but all I saw was this . . .

and this . . .

and this . . .

"Is that it?" I said. "*Two* pictures? You've had a whole year and you've only come up with *two* pictures? Honestly, Terry! Do you expect me to do *all* the work—the pictures as well as the writing?"

"Of course not," said Terry, "you can't *draw*."

"Yes I can!" I said. "Drawing is easy. It's coming up with the words that takes real skill."

"If you think drawing is so easy then let's have a competition," said Terry, handing me a pencil.

"No problem!" I said.

First we drew a knife.

"That's not a knife," said Terry. "*This* is a knife."

Next we drew a worm.

"That's not a worm," said Terry. "*This* is a worm."

Wow, my picture is so good the bird thinks it's real.

Next we drew a banana.

"That's not a banana," said Terry. "*This* is a banana."

"No," I said, "*that's* not a banana. *This* is a banana!"
I picked up the giant banana that Terry had made
the day before and charged at him.

"Put the giant banana down, Andy," said Terry,
backing away.

"I'll put it down," I said, "when you admit that
I'm a better drawer than you are."

"But you're not."

"Okay," I said, "then I'm sorry to inform you that
I'm going to have to whack you over the head with
this giant banana."

"Not if I can whack you first!" said Terry, snatching the banana from my hands and whacking me over the head with it.

That's when everything went black.

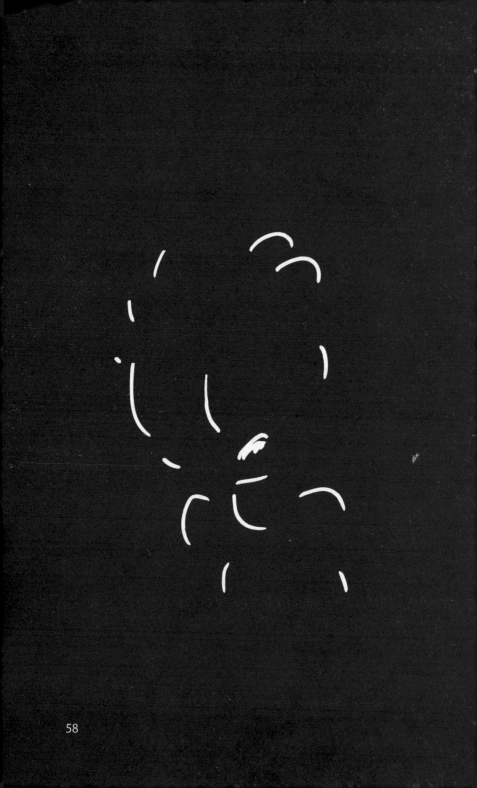

61

The next thing I knew I was soaking wet and Terry was kneeling in front of me holding an empty bucket.

"I'm so glad you're all right!" he said. "I thought I'd killed you!"

"So did I," I said. "I can't believe you whacked me with a giant banana!"

"But you were going to whack *me* with it."

"Two wrongs don't make a right, Terry," I reminded him.

"I suppose not," he said, "and I'm sorry. But look on the bright side. At least I saved your life by throwing a bucket of water in your face."

"But now I'm all wet!"

"Yes, but at least it's better than being dead."

"I'll tell you one thing," I said, "we're both as good as dead if we don't stop wasting time and get our book finished."

"You mean get our book *started*," said Terry. "Do you have anything in your writing folder?"

"Actually, I do have the start of a story," I said. "And it's a pretty good one, too."

"That's great," said Terry. "Let's see it!"

I grabbed my writing book and began turning the pages.

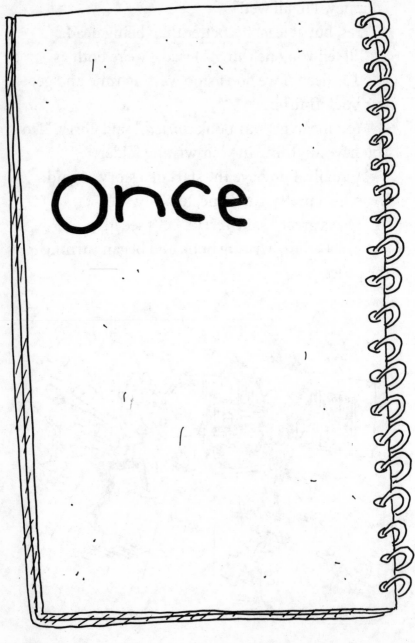

Once

upom

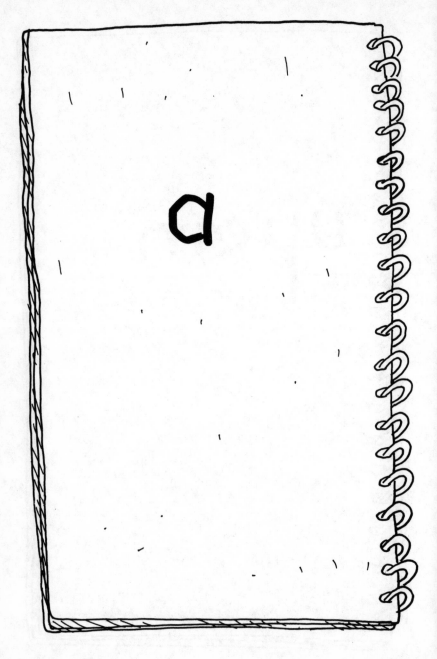

time

"Great start!" said Terry. "Action-packed! But what happens next?"

"I'm not sure," I said. "That's as far as I got."

"That's it?" said Terry. "Four words?!"

"Four *pages*," I said.

"Yeah, but it's still only *four words*," said Terry, "and one of them isn't even spelled right. I'm pretty sure it's 'upon,' not 'upom.'"

"Well excuse me, Mr. Roald Dahl!" I said. "If you know so much about story writing, why don't *you* write it?"

"Because it's time for my favorite TV show!" said Terry.

"What about our book?" I said.

"Why don't you write while I watch?"

"Because I can't write when the TV is on!" I said. "I can't concentrate!"

"Then come and watch it with me," said Terry, patting the beanbag beside him.

And that's why, instead of working on our book, we ended up wasting half an hour watching the world's dumbest dog on the world's dumbest TV show.

But don't just take my word for it.
See for yourself!

CHAPTER 6

THE BARKY THE BARKING DOG SHOW

THE END

CHAPTER 7

THE MONSTER MERMAID

See what I mean?

TV shows don't get much dumber than that.

"Okay, Terry," I said when it was finally over. "Let's get back to work."

"But it's time for my second favorite show," said Terry, "*Buzzy the Buzzing Fly!*"

"Oh no it's not," I said, grabbing the remote and turning off the TV.

"Oh yes it is," said Terry, snatching the remote out of my hand and turning it back on.

"Actually, I think you'll find that it's *not*," I said, picking up the TV and throwing it out of the treehouse. It landed with a crash on the ground below.

Terry shrugged.
"I guess you're right," he said.

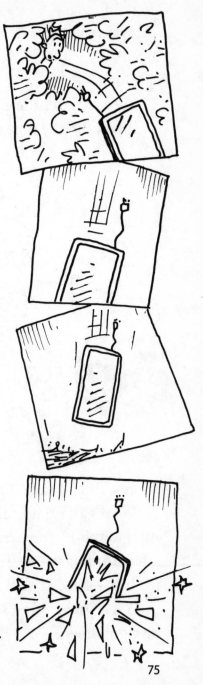

"Hey!" yelled a voice. "That almost landed on my head!"

Oops.

I peeped over the edge.

It was Bill the postman.

"Sorry, Bill!" I said. "It was an accident."

"That's all right," said Bill, chuckling. "Delivering mail to the 13-story treehouse is always an adventure! Is young Terry there? I've got a parcel for him—special delivery."

"YAY!" said Terry, sprinting for the ladder. "I'll be right down!"

He returned a few minutes later with a package.

"My sea-monkeys!" he yelled as he opened it.
"They've arrived at last!"

"Sea-monkeys?" I said. "What do you want them for? We've already got a perfectly good tank full of man-eating sharks!"

"But sea-monkeys are much better than man-eating sharks," said Terry. "Sea-monkeys have *three* eyes, they breathe through their *feet*, and they build vast underwater kingdoms! Sharks can't do any of that . . . sharks don't even *have* feet! I'm going to make my sea-monkeys come alive right now!"

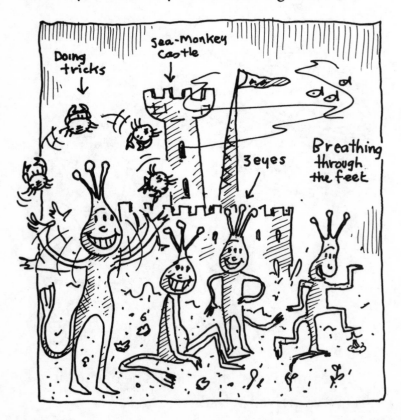

"Not so fast," I said. "We've got a book to write, remember?"

"I know!" said Terry. "And I promise I'll get to work right after I've hatched the sea-monkeys. They come to life instantly. All I have to do is add water. Please. *Please? PLEASE?!*"

"Okay," I said, "but hurry!"

"Sure thing!" said Terry, rushing to the elevator. "I'll be right back."

I waited for a long time . . .

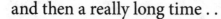

and then a really long time . . .

and then a really *really* long time . . .

but he didn't come back.

Eventually I found him down in the secret underground laboratory.

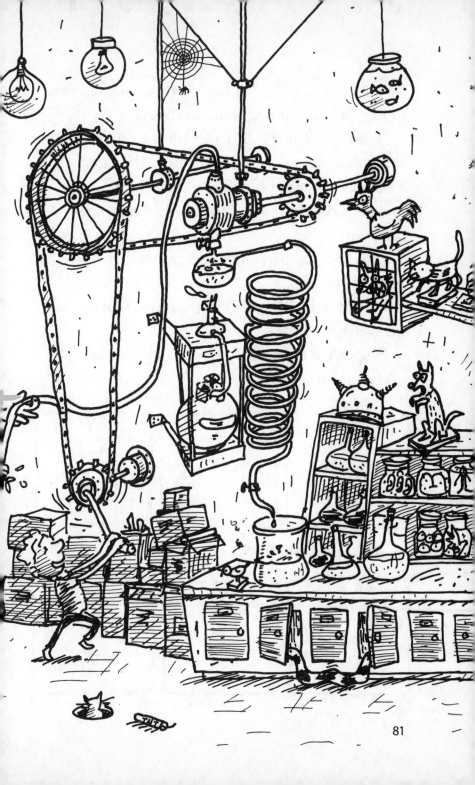

"What are you doing?" I said. "I thought you were supposed to be adding water to the eggs."

"I am!" said Terry. "I've just finished making the apparatus that will help me measure the exact amount of water I need. Too much and the sea-monkeys could drown. Too little and they could suffocate."

"But you said hatching the eggs would be *instant*!" I said.

"And it will be," said Terry, "just as soon as I add the water. Now stand back."

He pushed a button and the water dripped out of the machine, drop . . .

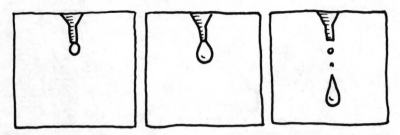

by painfully slow drop . . .

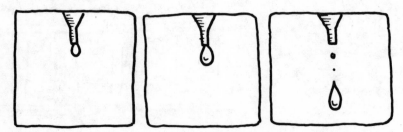

by even more painfully slow drop . . .

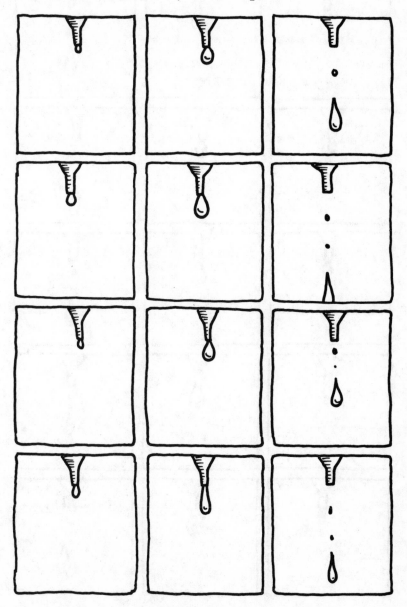

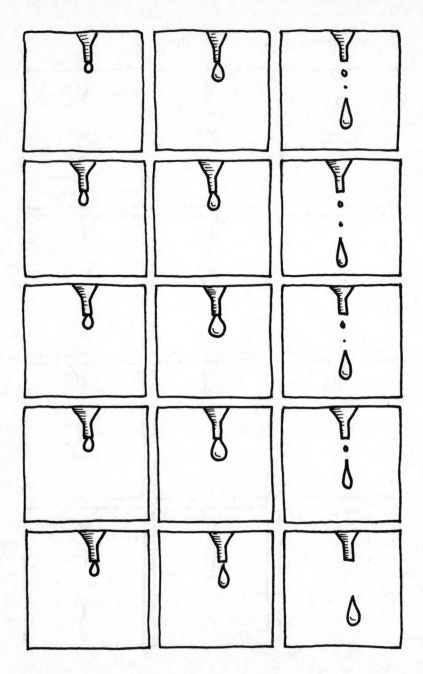

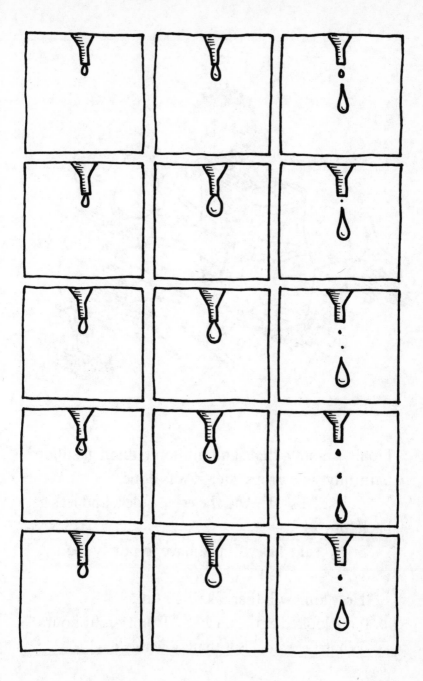

Finally, about a thousand million trillion gazillion painfully slow drops later, it was done.

"At last!" I said. "Add the eggs, quick, and let's get back to work."

"Sure," said Terry. "I just have to purify the water."

"How long will that take?" I said.

Terry looked at the packet. "Twenty-four hours."

"What?!" I said. "But that's a whole day!"

"Don't be silly, Andy," said Terry, laughing. "There aren't twenty-four hours in a day!"

"YES THERE ARE!" I shouted. "And if you think I'm going to let you waste any more time on these stupid sea-monkeys, then you're out of your tiny, pea-brained, numbskull-sized mind!"

BRAINS: A SIMPLE GUIDE

(THESE DRAWINGS ARE NOT TO SCALE)

"Watch your language, Andy," said Terry. "There might be children reading."

"I don't care *who* is reading," I said. "Put your sea-monkey eggs in that water right now or else I swear I'll shove that jar onto your head so hard that it will be stuck on there for the rest of your life! How would you like that?"

Terry thought about it for a moment.

89

"I don't think I'd like it at all," he said finally.
"I guess, under the circumstances, we can skip the water-purifying step and add the eggs straight away."

"Great thinking," I said.

Terry's hand was trembling as he poured the sea-monkey eggs into the jar.

He stirred it and held it up to the light.

"I've done it!" he shouted. "I'm a genius! I've created *life*!"

He was right.

Not about being a genius, of course, but there was definitely a bunch of newly hatched sea-monkeys bobbing around in the jar.

"Well, that's just great," I said. "Now can we get back to our book?"

"Not yet," said Terry. "I have to feed them one level scoop of official sea-monkey growth food."

I groaned. "Does that mean that now you have to build a one-level-scoop-of-official-sea-monkey-growth-food-dispensing-machine?"

"No need for that! They come with their own official sea-monkey growth food–dispensing utensil," said Terry as he sprinkled sea-monkey growth food from a plastic spoon into the top of the jar.

The food triggered a feeding frenzy. Well, in one sea-monkey, at least. It swam straight to it and sucked it all up before the others could get any.

"What a guts!" said Terry.

"Better put some more in," I said.

Terry measured out another spoonful and sprinkled it into the jar.

Once again the greedy sea-monkey ate it all . . . and then it started to grow.

Within seconds it doubled in size and then doubled in size again. Then it swam around the jar and ate *all* the other sea-monkeys!

It grew bigger . . .

and bigger . . .

and bigger.

"It's getting too big for the jar!" said Terry.

"Get a beaker!" I said. "A really big beaker!"

Terry darted away and returned with the biggest beaker we had.

"That ought to hold it," he said, as he tipped the sea-monkey from the jar into its new home.

But the sea-monkey kept right on growing. Soon
it was too big for the beaker, so we tipped it into
a bucket. But it quickly outgrew that as well.

"It's no use," said Terry. "We need something even
bigger!"

"How about the bath?" I said.

"I didn't know we had a bath!" said Terry.

"Yes," I said. "I've been meaning to talk to you
about that. It's in the bathroom."

"I didn't know we had a bath*room*!" said Terry.

"Just bring the bucket and follow me," I said.

"That is one *weird*-looking sea-monkey!" I said, when we'd finally got it into the bath.

"That's because I'm *not* a sea-monkey," said the weird-looking sea-monkey. "I am a *mermaid*!"

"A mermaid?" said Terry, looking like he was about to cry. "But mermaids are for *girls*! I ordered sea-monkeys!"

"It's not *my* fault," said the mermaid. "The eggs must have got mixed up at the factory. My name is Mermaidia, what's yours?"

"Terry," he said.

"That's a nice name for a merman," said Mermaidia.

"I'm not a merman," said Terry.

"Oh, I thought you were," said Mermaidia, gazing at Terry. "You're certainly good-looking enough to be one."

Terry blushed and giggled.

"Hello," I said. "I'm Andy."

"Uh-huh," said Mermaidia, not taking her eyes off Terry.

"I live here, too," I said.

"Uh-huh," said Mermaidia. "Why don't you run along now, Sandy? Terry and I would like to be alone."

"Yes," said Terry, dreamily.

"But what about our book?" I said. "When are we going to do that?"

But it was no use.

Neither of them were listening to me. They were just gazing into each other's eyes. It was quite embarrassing, actually.

I stepped out of the room and closed the door. The thing was, though, I could still hear what they were saying.

"You are so sweet," said Mermaidia. "I wish I could stay here with you!"

"But you can ... can't you?" said Terry.

"Alas, no," said Mermaidia. "I can't live in a bathtub forever."

"We've got a swimming pool!" said Terry. "It's see-through! You could live there!"

"But I need to live in the sea," said Mermaidia. "It's where I belong."

"Oh," said Terry sadly.

"I know!" said Mermaidia. "Why don't you come to live with me? We could live in my 13-story sand castle under the sea!"

"That would be nice," said Terry. "But I'm not a merman—I can't breathe underwater."

"There is a way, though," said Mermaidia. "When a human and a mermaid get married the human *becomes* a merman . . . and all we have to do to be married is kiss."

I should have rushed in and broken it up right then and there, but I didn't want them to know I'd been listening. And, besides, I was too late anyway. I shuddered as I heard the unmistakable sound of a human and a mermaid kissing.

"Oh, darling," crooned Mermaidia, "I'm *so* happy! Let's leave right away!"

"Okay," said Terry. "I've just got to say good-bye to Andy."

"All right, but hurry," sighed Mermaidia impatiently. "I don't know how much longer I can last in this bathwater."

I quickly hid as Terry came out of the bathroom.

He climbed down the ladder and started looking for me.

"Andy," he called. "I need to talk to you!"

I was about to go down and join him when I heard a strange gurgling sound coming from the bathroom. It sounded like Mermaidia was choking and, even though I didn't especially like her, I thought I should still see if she was all right. But as I entered the bathroom I caught sight of her reflection in the mirror. And what I saw was definitely *not* all right. In fact, it was definitely *all wrong*. Very, very wrong!

Mermaidia wasn't Mermaidia anymore. *She was a sea monster!*

How could I be so sure that she was a sea monster?

Well, for a start, there was her slimy sea-monstery skin . . .

and her slimy sea-monstery tentacles . . .

and her slimy sea-monstery stench . . .

. . . but, above all, I think it was the fact that she was saying, "Bathroom mirror, on the wall . . . who's the sneakiest *sea monster* of all?" that really clinched it for me.

You know when you see something so horrible that you want to look away but you can't? Well, this was *so* horrible that I had to get out my flip camera and record it!

And with that, the monster became Mermaidia
again and climbed back into the bathtub.

I stopped recording and rushed off to find
Terry.

He was down in the kitchen.

The marshmallow dispenser was shooting marshmallows into his mouth just as fast as he could swallow them.

"Guess what, Andy?" he mumbled with his mouth full.

"Um, let me see . . . you and Mermaidia got married and you're off to live in an underwater 13-story sand castle?"

Terry was amazed.

"How did you know?!"

"I heard the whole thing," I said. "And that's not all I heard—after you left I discovered that Mermaidia is not a mermaid at all . . . she's a sea monster!"

"That's a lie!" said Terry. "You're just jealous!"

"No, I'm not," I said. "Look at this!"

I pressed PLAY on my camera and handed it to him.

"Yikes!" said Terry. "What am I going to do?"

"Well, for a start," I said, "I think you should definitely break up with her. And pretty soon, too."

"Of course I will!" said Terry. "But what if she tries to eat me?"

"Calm down," I said. "I was just joking. For the moment there's no need to do anything. She doesn't know that *you* know that *she's* a sea monster . . ."

"*Oh yes I do,*" said a hideous gurgling voice behind us.

We turned to see "Mermaidia" sliming her way across the kitchen toward us.

"Go away!" said Terry, trying to hide behind me.

"But we're married, my darling," she said, extending her horrible face toward Terry.

"Don't kiss me!" he pleaded, his eyes wide in alarm.

"I'm not going to *kiss* you," she said. "I'm going to *eat* you . . . and your eavesdropping friend!"

"But I didn't mean to eavesdrop!" I said. "Can't you just let me off with a warning . . . or a small fine . . . or something?"

"I suppose I could," said Mermaidia, "it's just that I'm so *very* hungry. Being cooped up in a sea-monkey packet for so long gives one *such* an appetite!"

We backed away from Mermaidia until we were pressed up against the elevator doors. I felt around behind me, desperately trying to find the button to open the door as she slimed closer and closer.

Finally I found it! The doors slid open and we tumbled backward into the elevator.

Mermaidia roared as the doors slid shut.

"Phew!" said Terry. "I'm glad that's over!"

"Are you kidding?" I said, as we descended toward the laboratory. "That was only round one!"

"So what are we going to do now?"

"Well," I said, "this might be a dumb question but can the banana-enlarger work in reverse?"

"You mean as a banana-*shrinker*?" said Terry. "Sure. It's simply a matter of reversing the polarity . . . but how are shrunken bananas going to help us fight a sea monster?"

"They're not," I explained as the elevator doors opened into the lab. "And we're not going to *fight* a sea monster. We're going to *shrink* it! But you're going to have to work fast. Your wife will be here any second."

"Don't remind me!" said Terry, making a dash for the enlarger.

I listened as the elevator rose through the trunk back to the main level. Mermaidia had obviously summoned it and would be here any moment.

"One sea-monster shrinker ready for action!" said Terry.

"Just in time!" I said.

I stood as close to the elevator as I dared.
The doors slid open and Mermaidia oozed into the
room.

"Ah, there you are," she gurgled. "I can't believe you
really thought you were going to get away from me!
You humans are so stupid."

"And you're nothing but an overgrown sea-
monkey!" I taunted her as I backed across the lab
toward the shrinker, hoping she would follow.

"I am not a sea-*monkey*," she shrieked as she
slimed her way toward me. "I'm a sea *monster*!
And just for that I'm going to eat *you* first."

"Oh no you're not," I said.

"Oh yes I am," she said as she touched the tip of
my nose with one of her stinking black tentacles.

"No, you're really not!" I shouted, jumping clear. "Now, Terry!"

Terry fired up the shrinker and blasted her with the ray.

Mermaidia screamed in rage as she began to shrink before our eyes.

"I'M SHRINKING!" she screamed as she grew smaller and smaller.

Soon she was no larger—and no more dangerous—than a jellybean. She lay on the floor between us, ranting in a tiny, high voice.

"She was the worst sea-monkey *ever*!" said Terry. "I've got a good mind to send her back to the factory."

"We're going to send her back all right," I said. "But not to the factory—back to the sea where she belongs. In fact, I'm going to do it right now. Unless you'd prefer to."

"No, I don't think I can," said Terry.

"Fine," I said.

I picked her up with a pair of tweezers, dropped her into the toilet, and pushed full flush.

Twice. I wasn't taking any chances.

When I came out Terry was wiping away a tear.

"I can only guess how sad you must feel," I said, putting my arm around him, "but try to look on the bright side."

"What bright side?"

"Now we can get on with our book!"

CHAPTER 8

THE BIG BUBBLE

We took the elevator up to the main deck and sat down at the table.

"Okay," I said, "where were we up to? Oh that's right . . . 'Once upon a time.' Now let me see . . . Once upon a time there was a . . . a . . . a . . . help me out here, Terry! Once upon a time there was a . . . *what*?"

"A *whatever*," sighed Terry. "I don't care. I can't work. I'm too sad. I know Mermaidia was a sea monster but I really liked her when she was a mermaid."

"How about a marshmallow?" I said. "Would that help? I'll call the machine over."

"Nah," said Terry. "I'm tired of marshmallows."

"Maybe you just need a change," I said. "How about some popcorn?"

Terry shrugged.

"We can pop it with the lid off," I said.

Terry shrugged again. "Okay."

I filled the popcorn-maker up and turned it on.

We waited . . .

and waited . . .

and waited . . .

and just when we thought it was never going to pop, suddenly .... IT DID!

We ran around and caught as much of it in our mouths as we could until we couldn't eat any more.

"That was a great idea, Andy!" said Terry. "But now I'm *really* thirsty."

"Some lemonade will fix that," I said. "I'll start the fountain."

Did I mention that we have a lemonade fountain?
Well, we do. It's just like a regular fountain but
instead of water it has lemonade. Any flavor
you want as long as it's red, orange, lemon, cola,
or tutti-frutti (which is all the flavors mixed
together).

Fake grass

We sat in the lemonade fountain for a long time.
And when I say "a long time," I mean probably a lot
longer than we really should have.

"Oops, excuse me!" said Terry, covering his mouth with his hand.

But before I could excuse him I burped even louder.

"No, excuse *me*," I said.

Terry burped again, even louder this time.

"Well, you certainly sound like you're feeling better," I said.

"*Much* better," said Terry. "All I need now is some bubblegum!"

He climbed out of the lemonade fountain, went over to the bubblegum dispenser, reeled off a long strip, and shoved it all in to his mouth.

"Mmm, that's good," Terry mumbled as he chewed.
"Hey, I've got a great idea, Andy—watch this!"
   Terry chewed and burped . . .

and burped and chewed . . .

and blew and burped . . .

and burped and blew . . .

until he had blown the biggest bubble I had ever
seen. The bubble was so big that I couldn't even see
Terry anymore.

"That's enough!" I said. "It's getting too big!"

But Terry couldn't hear me. And the reason for
that was because the bubble had become so big
that it had completely surrounded him! He was
inside his own burp-gas-filled bubblegum bubble!

"Hey, this is really fun!" said Terry as he floated around in his bubble.

"Be careful," I said.

"What could possibly go wrong?" he said.

And then he began to float higher and higher up into the air. "HELP!" he cried.

"Don't worry!" I called to him as he floated up, up and away from the treehouse, "I'll save you!"

I took a running jump at the closest vine and swung out as far as I could to try to catch the bubble. It was a good swing, but not quite good enough. My hand closed on thin air and Terry continued to float away, higher and higher into the sky.

There was only one thing to do. I grabbed my golf clubs and raced up to the observation deck. I figured now would be a great time to work on my golf swing . . . and, of course, to try to pop Terry's bubble at the same time.

I gave it my best shot but I didn't have any luck on my first attempt . . .

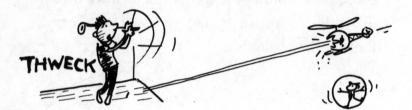

or on my second . . .

or even on my third . . .

but my fourth attempt was a bull's-eye!

The bubble burst apart,
which was
both good
and bad.
Good because
Terry was
no longer trapped
in a bubble
full of burp gas,
but *bad*
because now he
was plummeting
toward the ground
without a parachute
. . . or even . . .
a crash helmet.

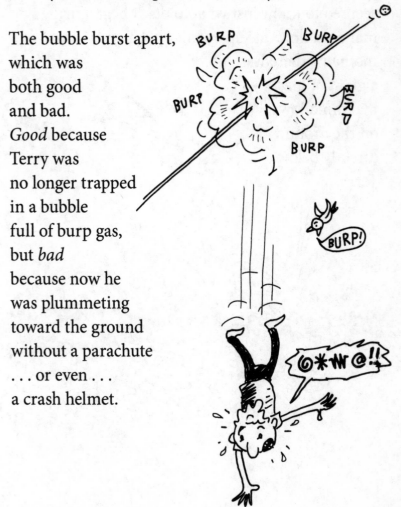

Luckily, however, the marshmallow machine
seemed to know just what to do. It began firing
marshmallows at supersonic speed and within
moments there was
a giant pillow of
marshmallows
on the ground
directly below
Terry.

He landed right in the middle and bounced many
times before finally coming to rest. It looked kind
of fun . . . well . . . a *lot* of fun, actually.

I helped Terry out of the marshmallow pile and dusted him off.

"That was the best fun *ever*!" he said with a big grin. "You should try it!"

"I would," I said, "but we've got a book to write, remember?"

"Oh yeah," said Terry. "I forgot."

We rode the elevator
back up to
the main deck.
This was really it.
No more distractions.
No more excuses.
No more flying cats,
giant banana attacks,
barking dogs,
pretend mermaids,
evil sea monsters,
popcorn parties,
lemonade guzzling,
burp-gas-filled
bubblegum bubbles,
or marshmallow
trampolines . . .
we were just going
to do our book.

We sat down at the table.

"So, where were we up to?" I said.

"'Once *upom* a time' I think," said Terry.

"Very funny," I said. "Now let me see . . . Once upon a time there was a . . . *what*?"

"Finger!" said Terry.

"Finger?" I said.

"Yes!" said Terry. "Why don't we put *your* beginning and *my* drawing together? You know, like, 'Once upon a time . . . there was a finger. But let's not make it an ordinary finger—let's make it a *super* finger!' Like this."

"That's crazy!" I said.

"Oh," said Terry, looking disappointed.

"So crazy it might just work!" I added.

"Then what are we waiting for?" said Terry, beaming. "Let's do it!"

So, there we were.

Me writing.

Terry drawing.

It was turning out pretty good, too, as you can see . . .

CHAPTER 9

THE ADVENTURES OF SUPERFINGER

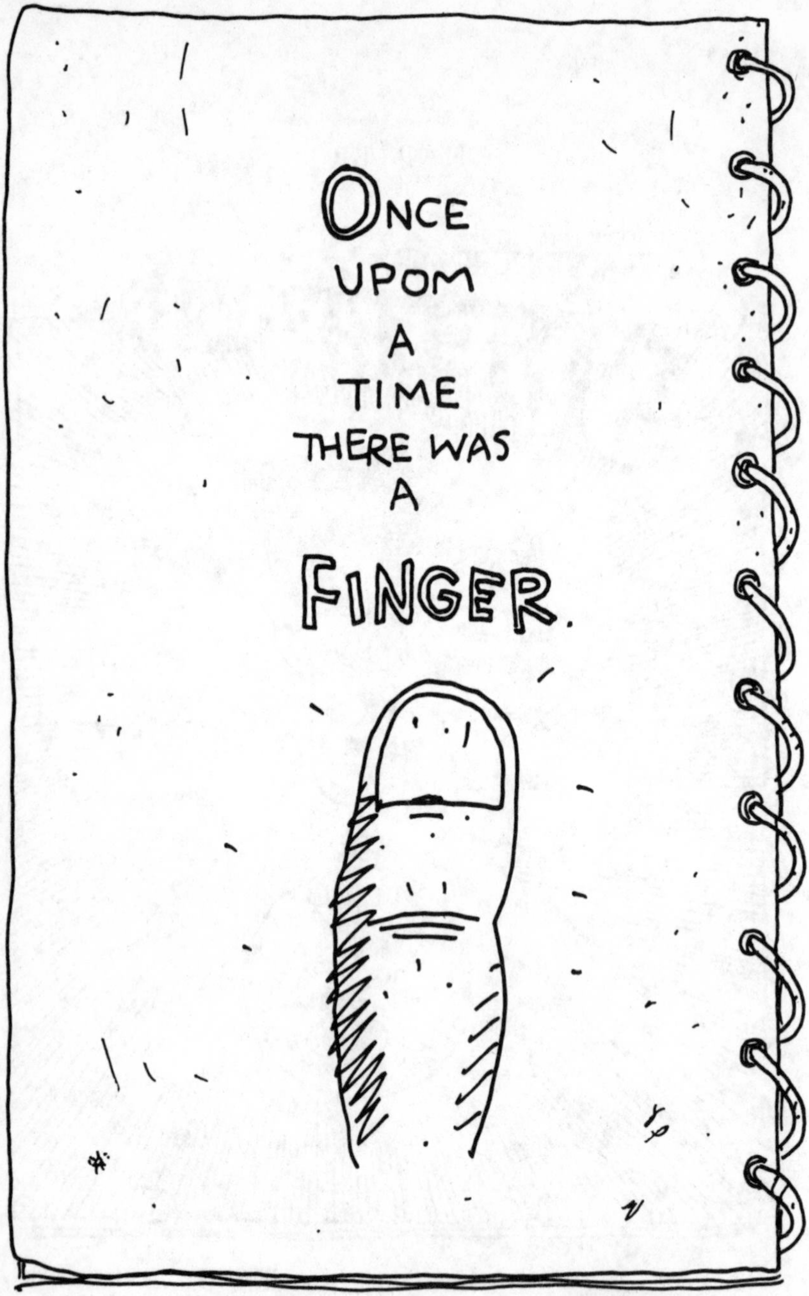
ONCE
UPOM
A
TIME
THERE WAS
A
FINGER.

SUPERFINGER HELPED THE HELPLESS...
Drat! I'll never get this package tied... if only I had an extra finger!
I'LL HELP YOU SOLVE THIS KNOTTY PROBLEM.
Thanks, Super-finger!

CHAPTER 10

THE 13-STORY MONKEY HOUSE

"Well, what do you think?" I said.

"It's great!" said Terry. "It's the best story we've done all year!"

"It's the *only* story we've done all year," I reminded him. "Come on, let's write the next one."

We were just about to get started when the doorbell rang.

"Hey, Terry," called Bill. "Got another package for you."

"Oh great!" said Terry. "It must be my replacement sea-monkeys!"

"Replacements?" I said.

"Yeah," said Terry. "I rang the sea-monkey company and told them what happened. They said they'd send some more eggs. They were very sorry."

"*They* were sorry?" I said. "*You'll* be the one who's sorry if you get another sea monster!"

But Terry wasn't listening to me. He was already on his way to the front door.

I waited for a while but Terry didn't return.
I figured he must have gone straight to the lab to
make his new sea-monkeys.

So I went down to see and, sure enough, there
he was.

"I've done it!" he said,
holding a jar
up to the light.
"These are
definitely sea-monkeys!"

"Congratulations," I said. "Are you happy now?"
Terry shrugged. "Nah, not really," he said.
"Sea-monkeys aren't that interesting after all."
"Never mind," I said. "Let's get back to work."

Soon we were back at our table, about to start work on the next story, when we heard a loud crash.

"What was that?" said Terry.

"I don't know," I said. "But it sounds like it came from the lab."

We both jumped up and rushed to the elevator.

As the doors to the laboratory slid open we were greeted with a scene of total chaos. There were monkeys everywhere and they were wrecking everything!

162

163

They were swinging and leaping and chasing each other all over the laboratory. The noise was deafening.

"Oh no!" said Terry. "I hope my sea-monkeys are all right!"

"They *are* your sea-monkeys!" I yelled, pointing to the empty jar on the floor. "Except they're not *sea*-monkeys—they're *monkey* monkeys! That stupid company has sent you the wrong sort of eggs again!"

"But I *hate* monkeys!" said Terry.

"Not as much as I do," I said.

"They're getting into the elevator!" said Terry.

"Oh great!" I said. "Now they're going to wreck the rest of the treehouse!"

We watched helplessly as the doors closed and the elevator rose through the trunk back to the main level.

In the time it took for the elevator to come down again and take us back up, the monkeys had created complete havoc on every single story of the treehouse.

There were monkeys in the bowling alley!

There were monkeys in the bathroom!

There were monkeys in the swimming pool!

There were monkeys in the kitchen!

There were monkeys on the observation deck!

There were monkeys *everywhere*!

"Watch out!" I shouted.

A bunch of monkeys were riding the marshmallow machine straight at us and firing marshmallows at our heads.

At the same time another bunch of monkeys were swinging toward us on a vine.

"Duck!" I yelled.

We bobbed down.

The monkeys on the vine collided with the monkeys on the marshmallow machine.

Monkeys and marshmallows and bits of the marshmallow machine went flying in all directions.

But the collision didn't seem to bother them a bit. They picked themselves up and began pelting us with anything they could get their dirty little monkey paws on.

"What are we going to do, Andy?" said Terry.

"Definitely *not* order any more sea-monkeys," I said.

"Yeah, but *before* that," said Terry.

"Whack them with the giant banana?" I suggested. "It's just there." I pointed to where it was lying on the floor near Terry.

"But you said two wrongs don't make a right," said Terry.

"They do when there's monkeys involved!" I said.

Terry picked up the giant banana and, holding it like a baseball bat, began whacking back the marshmallows, pens, pencils, erasers, paintbrushes, paints, and monkey poop being hurled in our direction. And then he began knocking the monkeys right out of the tree!

But then the strangest thing happened. As fast as Terry could knock the monkeys out of the tree they climbed back up again. But not to continue their crazy rampage . . . it was simply to sit and watch him. Or, more to the point, to watch the giant banana. As Terry swung, more and more monkeys came to sit quietly in front of him.

"Why are they just sitting there?" said Terry.

"They seem to *really* like the banana," I said. "Just keep waving it slowly back and forth . . . I think you're hypnotizing them."

Sure enough, Terry soon had the entire gang of monkeys under the spell of the giant banana.

"What do I do now?" he said.

"Lead them up to the top of the tree," I said, "and put them in the giant catapult."

"Of course!" said Terry. "Why didn't I think of that?"

"You did, actually," I reminded him.

Terry had originally designed the catapult as a garbage-disposal unit but we had to stop using it for that because we got too many complaints from our neighbors.

WHY WE HAD TO STOP USING OUR CATAPULT AS A GARBAGE DISPOSAL UNIT.

SPLAT! ?!!

For a while we used it to play tricks on each other . . .

but these days we mostly use it for getting rid of
unwanted guests . . . in this case, *monkeys*!

I followed Terry as he led the monkeys up to the
top of the tree and helped him load them into the
catapult.

"You'd better put the giant banana on board, too,"
I said, "just in case they come back looking for it."

"Done," said Terry, strapping the banana to the
mesmerized monkeys.

"All right," I said. "Prepare to launch!"

The enormous arm of the catapult hurled the
monkeys and the giant banana up,

up,

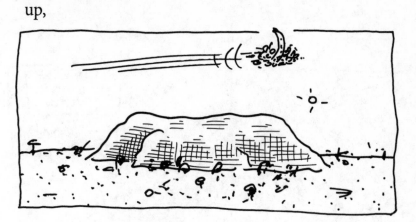

up into the air and far,

far,

far away.

"We did it!" said Terry.

"Yes," I said, "now we can get back to finishing our book!"

CHAPTER 11

THE GIANT GORILLA

But before we could get back to finishing our book we had to clean up the mess the monkeys had made.

Finally, after about a thousand million trillion gazillion years, we had everything back to normal and were ready to start work again.

I had just finished writing the words, "Once upom another time," and Terry had just finished pointing out that I had misspelled "upon" again when the table began shaking.

"Quit shaking the table!" I said.

"I'm not shaking the table," said Terry. "I thought *you* were shaking the table."

"I'm not shaking the table!" I said, as the treehouse began to sway.

"Quit swaying the treehouse!" said Terry.

"I'm *not* swaying the treehouse," I said. "I thought *you* were swaying the treehouse."

"It's not *me*," said Terry. "I think it's that giant gorilla down there."

"But why would a giant gorilla be shaking our tree?" I said.

"Beats me," said Terry. "It's not like it's a *banana* tree."

"Of course!" I said. "That's it! To the gorilla it *is* a banana tree . . . a *giant banana* tree!"

"Huh?" said Terry.

"Isn't it obvious?" I said. "The giant banana we catapulted must have landed on a distant tropical island . . .

where the giant gorilla lives . . .

and it found the giant banana and ate it . . .

and loved it so much that it made a boat out of the giant banana peel . . .

and used its giant nostrils to track the giant banana's scent all the way back here . . .

and is now shaking our tree in the mistaken belief that it's a *giant banana tree*."

"It seems a *little* far-fetched," said Terry. "All that trouble for a banana?"

"A *giant* banana," I reminded him. "With extra giant-banana flavor."

Just then we heard the unmistakable roar of a giant gorilla that has traveled across the ocean in a giant banana peel boat in search of giant bananas.

"I think you could be right," said Terry. "It would certainly explain why it's here, shaking our tree. What are we going to do?"

"Give it more giant bananas, of course!" I said.

"We can't!" said Terry. "The monkeys broke the banana-enlarger!"

"Can't you fix it?"

"Maybe, but it would take too long!" said Terry. "They've completely pulled it apart!"

"Well we've got to do *something*!" I said. "Before it shakes the treehouse to pieces!"

"BANANA!" roared the giant gorilla. "BANANA!"

"There are no bananas here!" shouted Terry.
"Well, there was, but not anymore!"

"BANANA!" roared the gorilla in response.

"It's no use," I said. "Apart from the word 'banana,' I don't think it speaks English."

And then, just when we thought the day couldn't get any crazier, a white stretch limousine pulled up at our front door and a chauffeur in a fancy uniform got out and rang our doorbell.

"We're up here!" I called down to him.

"Which one of you is Terry?" he said.

"Me!" said Terry.

"Well," said the chauffeur, "I'm very pleased to inform you that you have won first prize in the Barky the Barking Dog drawing competition with your drawing of Barky at the beach."

"Wow, that's so exciting," said Terry. "What do I win?"

"You get to meet Barky," said the chauffeur.

"When?" said Terry.

"Right now!" said the chauffeur, opening the back door of the limousine.

"This is great!" said Terry. "Barky's here! Not only do I get to meet him, but he can save us—*and* the treehouse!"

"And how *exactly* is he going to do that?" I said.

"By barking, of course!" said Terry.

Right on cue, Barky emerged from the limo and began barking at the giant gorilla.

He barked,

and barked,

and barked.

And then the giant gorilla lifted up one of its
gigantic feet and stomped on him.

We watched as the chauffeur scooped Barky up and carried him to the limo.

"Do you think he's okay?" said Terry.

"Well, he's still barking," I said.

"I didn't even really get to meet him," sighed Terry.

Meanwhile, the gorilla wasted no time in getting back to shaking the tree, only this time even harder than before.

"Oh no," said Terry. "We really *are* in trouble. Even Barky couldn't save us. What are we going to do?"

"Say good-bye to the treehouse," I said, "and say hello to the monkey house. Without the treehouse we'll have nowhere to live and nowhere to write books."

"I *hate* monkeys," said Terry. "*And* giant gorillas."

"Well, you've only got yourself to blame," I said. "If you hadn't sent away for sea-monkeys or fooled around with giant bananas in the first place, none of this would ever have happened!"

But Terry wasn't listening to me.

He was looking up into the sky.

"Can you hear that?" he said.

"You mean the sound of a giant gorilla destroying the treehouse?" I said. "Yep! Coming through, loud and clear!"

"*No,*" said Terry. "The sound of a flying cat. It's Silky! She's come back! And she's not alone!"

CHAPTER 12

THE DAY SILKY
SAVED THE DAY

I looked up. Terry was right!

Flying cats!

A whole bunch of them . . . 13 to be exact, with
Silky in the lead!

They were flying in formation, coming in low
and fast, like fighter jets.

"Oh, great," I said. "As if a giant gorilla wasn't bad enough, now we're being attacked by a flock of flying cats!"

"How do you know they're attacking us?" said Terry. "Maybe *they* want giant bananas, too."

"Cats don't eat bananas!" I said. "Everybody knows that. Besides, they look angry, not hungry!"

"Maybe it's the gorilla they're after," said Terry. "Look how scared it is!"

Terry had a point. The gorilla was no longer shaking the tree. It was staring at the cats, its fur bristling. It roared loudly, but if the cats were worried they didn't show it. They were definitely taking aim at the gorilla.

We braced ourselves for a 13-flying-cats-and-one-giant-gorilla collision.

But it never came.

At the last possible moment the cats separated
into two groups, flew past the gorilla, and soared
up into the sky, where they re-formed into a
menacing circle high above us.

That's when the gorilla started to climb the tree.

"There are no giant bananas up here!" shouted Terry. "We already told you that!"

"I don't think it's after giant bananas anymore," I said. "I think it's getting into a better position to fight the cats."

The gorilla climbed higher . . .

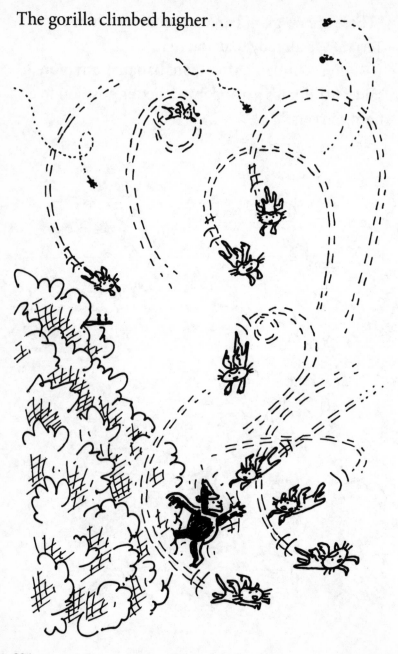

and higher . . .

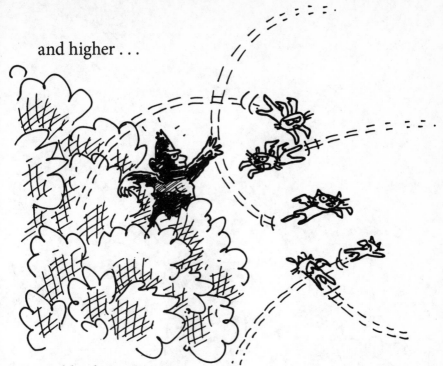

and higher . . .

205

until it was standing at the top of the tree. It beat its enormous chest and roared at the flying cats, which continued to attack and torment it.

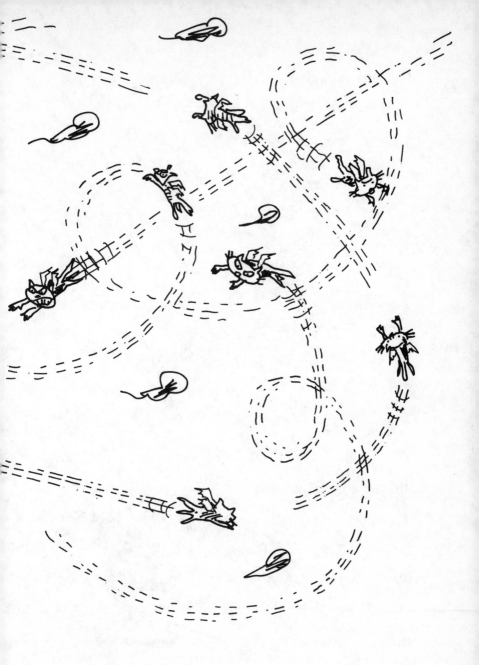

The cats swooped . . .

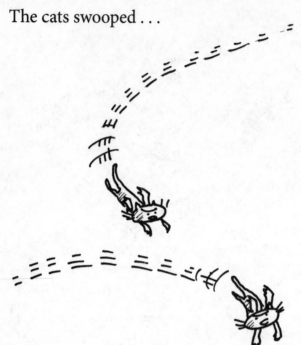

and the gorilla swiped.

Occasionally, the gorilla would strike the cats and send them crashing to the ground, but they always landed on their feet and rejoined the battle just as quickly as they'd left it.

Eventually, the 13 ferocious flying cats became too much for the gorilla. It lost its grip, fell out of the tree . . .

and crashed to the ground with a sickening thud.

But the flying cats still weren't finished with the
gorilla. Before it could get up they swooped down,
sunk their claws deep into its fur, and lifted it into
the air. Then they carried it away.

"Well, it looks like Silky and her pals saved the day!" said Terry. "If I hadn't turned her into a flying cat the treehouse would have been destroyed for sure!"

I was about to point out that the only reason the treehouse was in danger in the first place was because of him, his sea-monkeys, and his stupid giant banana, but at that moment the doorbell rang.

"Oh no," I said, "not *more* sea-monkeys! Terry, how could you?!"

But Terry didn't answer. He was already gone.

CHAPTER 13

THE END

I raced Terry, determined to stop him from hatching another bunch of eggs that might threaten our treehouse, not to mention our lives.

But it wasn't Bill the postman at the door.

It was Jill!

She was panting as if she'd run the whole way over. "Was that Silky I saw," she said, "flying away from your treehouse with a giant gorilla?"

"Yes," said Terry.

I elbowed him hard. "He means no," I said.

"Yes, that's right," said Terry. "I mean no."

Jill frowned. "I'm sure that was Silky."

"But isn't Silky white?" I said. "All those cats were yellow. And they were flying. Does Silky fly? You didn't mention it on your poster."

"Well, she doesn't *usually*," said Jill, "but one of those cats was Silky. I'm sure of it. I'd recognize her anywhere. And you two know something, I can tell. You'd better start talking . . . and fast."

"I'm sorry," I said, "but it wasn't my fault! It was Terry. He painted Silky yellow and turned her into a canary—well, a catnary, I guess—and then she flew away! I'm really, *really* sorry."

"A *catnary*?" said Jill slowly. "Terry turned Silky into a *catnary*?"

"Yes, and like I said, I *tried* to stop him . . ."

"But I'm so glad you didn't!" said Jill.

"Huh?" I said. "You don't *mind*?"

"Not at all!" said Jill. "In fact, it's fantastic! I've been really wanting to get a canary but I was worried that Silky would eat it. Having a flying cat is like having the best of both pets! Thank you, Terry!"

"You're welcome," said Terry. "If you'd like any of your other animals converted, you know where to bring them."

"Thanks," said Jill. "I'll definitely think about it. Meanwhile, I'd better get home and put out some birdseed for Silky and her new friends."

After she left, Terry clapped his hands together. "Well, that all turned out pretty well, don't you think?"

"I guess so," I said, "except for one small thing."

"What's that?"

"WE

STILL

HAVEN'T

WRITTEN

OUR

BOOK!"

"There's no need to shout, Andy," said Terry. "Just relax. It will all be okay."

"In what sense can I *possibly* relax and how can it all *possibly* be okay?" I said. "We still have *no book* and it's due in tomorrow. How are we ever going to think all the stories up in time, let alone write and illustrate them?"

"Easy," said Terry. "We don't have to think *anything* up. We've just lived through a *really* interesting day. All we have to do is write it all down, draw some pictures, and we'll have our book!"

You know, I'm much smarter than Terry, but sometimes I get this really weird feeling that he is actually much smarter than me.

"That's a crazy idea," I said.

"Oh," sighed Terry, disappointed.

"*So* crazy," I said, "it just might work!"

"What are we waiting for then?" said Terry. "Let's get started!"

And so we sat down and wrote and drew . . .

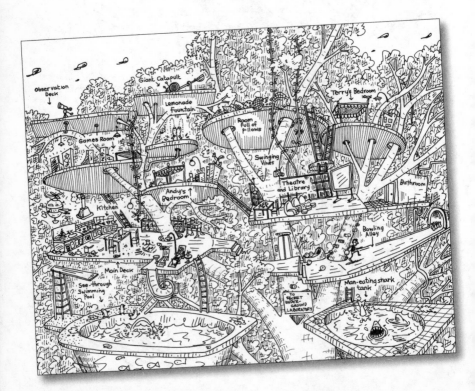

and drew . . .

But I needn't have worried. The cat didn't fall. Two little wings popped out of its back, and then it tweeted and flew away.

I started to explain to Terry that you can't turn a cat into a canary just by painting it yellow but he said, "Yes, you can—watch this!" and carried the dripping cat to the edge of the deck.

"No!" I yelled, as Terry held the cat out in mid-air ... and let it go.

22

"See?" said Terry, turning to me in triumph. "I told you so!"

23

and wrote . . .

CHAPTER 3

THE MISSING CAT

It was Jill, our neighbor. She lives on the other side of the forest in a house full of animals. She's got two dogs, a goat, three horses, four goldfish, one cow, six rabbits, two guinea pigs, one camel, one donkey, and one cat.

We watched the cat ... I mean canary ... actually, I think I mean *catnary* ... until it flew out of sight. Then the doorbell rang.

26

27

and wrote . . .

As soon as Jill left I turned to Terry. "We've *got* to find that cat!" I said.

"You mean *canary*," said Terry.

"Whatever!" I said. "We've got to find her."

But before we could even begin looking for her the video-phone rang. (Yes, we've got one of those as well—and it's 3D!)

"Maybe that's Silky now," said Terry.

"Don't be stupid," I said. "Cats can't use phones."

"Maybe they can," said Terry. "You said they couldn't turn into canaries and you were wrong about that!"

CHAPTER 4

THE BIG RED NOSE

We raced back upstairs. A big red nose filled the video-phone screen. Uh-oh. It was Mr. Big Nose, our publisher. And he was angry. I could tell this because his nose was even bigger—and redder—than usual.

and drew . . .

"No," I said,"*that's* not a banana. *This* is a banana!" I picked up the giant banana that Terry had made the day before and charged at him.

"Put the giant banana down, Andy," said Terry, backing away.

"I'll put it down,"I said,"when you admit that I'm a better drawer than you are."

"But you're not."

"Okay," I said, "then I'm sorry to inform you that I'm going to have to whack you over the head with this giant banana."

"Not if I can whack you first!" said Terry, snatching the banana from my hands and whacking me over the head with it.

That's when everything went black.

and drew . . .

THE END

and wrote . . .

I stood as close to the elevator as I dared. The doors slid open and Mermaidia oozed into the room.

"Ah, there you are," she gurgled. "I can't believe you really thought you were going to get away from me! You humans are so stupid."

"And you're nothing but an overgrown sea-*monkey*!" I taunted her as I backed across the lab toward the shrinker, hoping she would follow.

"I am not a sea-*monkey*," she shrieked as she slimed her way toward me. "I'm a sea *monster*! And just for that I'm going to eat *you* first."

"Oh no you're not," I said.

"Oh yes I am," she said as she touched the tip of my nose with one of her stinking black tentacles.

"No, you're really not!" I shouted, jumping clear. "Now, Terry!"

Terry fired up the shrinker and blasted her with the ray.

Mermaidia screamed in rage as she began to shrink before our eyes.

and drew . . .

Terry burped again, even louder this time.

"Well, you certainly sound like you're feeling better," I said.

"*Much* better," said Terry. "All I need now is some bubblegum!"

He climbed out of the lemonade fountain, went over to the bubblegum dispenser, reeled off a long strip, and shoved it all in to his mouth.

"Mmm, that's good," Terry mumbled as he chewed. "Hey, I've got a great idea, Andy—watch this!"

Terry chewed and burped . . .

and burped and chewed . . .

and wrote . . .

and wrote . . .

and drew . . .

and drew . . .

until exactly 4.45 p.m. the next day.

"We've done it!" I yelled.

"But it's quarter to five," said Terry. "How are we going to get it to Mr. Big Nose on time? Our deadline is five o'clock . . . we'll *never* make it!"

"Oh yes we will," I said.

"But how?"

"I don't know," I said, "but we'll think of something."

That's when we heard it.

A jingling noise.

Terry jumped up. "It's Santa Claus!" he said. "Quick, get the stockings, hang them up, and pretend we're asleep!"

"But it's not Christmas Eve," I said. "In fact, it's not even Christmas!"

We went to the edge of the deck and this is what we saw:

Jill was flying through the sky toward us in a pram drawn by Silky and the other flying cats.

"Check out my flying-cat sleigh," she said as she hovered in mid-air beside us. "Want to come for a ride?"

"We can't," I said. "We're busy. We're trying to figure out how to get our book to Mr. Big Nose in the city by five o'clock."

"*I* could take you," said Jill. "These flying cats are really fast! Come on! Climb aboard!"

And so we did.

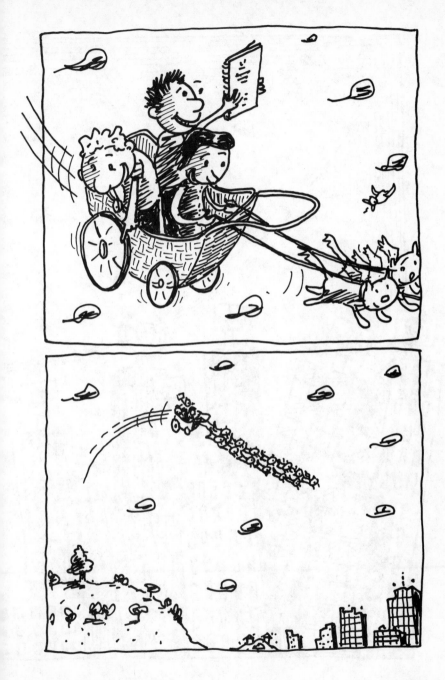

231

And that's how we got the book to Mr. Big Nose on time . . .

and then he published it . . .

and it was delivered to bookshops . . .

libraries . . .

digital e-reading devices . . .

and even transferred direct into people's brains via direct-to-brain information-delivery technology helmets* . . .

*Direct-to-brain information-delivery technology is a direct-to-brain information-delivery system so technologically advanced that Terry and I haven't even invented it yet.

and then *you* read it
and we all lived
happily ever after!*

*Unless, of course, your life was tragically cut short as a result of having your brain fried by one of our prototype direct-to-brain information-delivery technology helmets.

THE END

Andy Griffiths lives in a 13-story treehouse with his friend Terry and together they write funny books, just like the one you're holding in your hands right now. Andy writes the words and Terry draws the pictures. If you'd like to know more, read this book.

Terry Denton lives in a 13-story treehouse with his friend Andy and together they write funny books, just like the one you're holding in your hands right now. Terry draws the pictures and Andy writes the words. If you'd like to know more, read this book.

Watch out for

THE 26-STORY TREEHOUSE

Coming soon!

Visit Andy and Terry in their newly
expanded treehouse, which now features
13 brand-new stories, including a bumper car
rink, a skate ramp, a mud-fighting arena,
an anti-gravity chamber, an ice cream parlor
with 78 flavors (run by an ice cream-serving
robot called Edward Scooperhands), and
the Maze of Doom—a maze so complicated
that nobody who has gone in has ever
come out again. . . . Well, not yet, anyway.
So, what are you waiting for? Come on up!

Get ready for more
LAUGH ATTACKS

Written by Andy Griffiths
Illustrated by Terry Denton

978-0-312-36787-9

978-0-312-36788-6

978-0-312-36789-3

978-0-312-36790-9

Thank you for reading
this FEIWEL AND FRIENDS book.
The Friends who made

possible are:

Jean Feiwel, Publisher
Liz Szabla, Editor in Chief
Rich Deas, Creative Director
Holly West, Associate Editor
Dave Barrett, Executive Managing Editor
Nicole Liebowitz Moulaison, Production Manager
Lauren A. Burniac, Editor
Anna Roberto, Assistant Editor

Find out more about our authors and artists
and our future publishing at
mackids.com.

Our books are friends for life